I0580394

Santos CS Bermejo

The Medway Tales

"Do not shelter your children from the difficulties of life,
rather teach them to overcome them".

Louis Pasteur

"We are like dwarfs on the shoulders of giants,
so that we can see more than they,
and things at a greater distance".

Bernard of Chartres (AD 1130)

INDEX

PROLOGUE

To grown-ups:

The concept of **children's literature** has always meant, to me, a way of observing the world, understanding the core of reality, and explaining the aspects of life.

Since I was a child, I've found in storytelling, fables, and parables a vast reservoir of wisdom and a privileged vessel for passing on knowledge and culture.

While it's true that, originally, classics like "Gulliver's Travels," "Treasure Island," or "Platero and I" were specifically created for adults, the target audience gradually shifted with the emergence of the Modern Age and the recognition of childhood, adolescence, and youth as crucial stages in human development.

Timeless themes, such as epic adventures and the exploration of uncharted territories, later evolved into themes more focused on overcoming fears, the concept of freedom, aspirations, the world of dreams and desires, the transmission of values, and, more recently, the entire realm of mental health, emotions, and their management.

In either case, my engagement with children's literature has consistently served as a means through which I have been able to question and, subsequently, challenge significant and foundational pillars of reality as we know it. It has paved the way to explore individual personal life and its relationship with society.

I must admit that it is not always to my liking to see that children's literature is also instrumentalized, on certain occasions, and used with the intention of creating followers or disciples, in the hands of one or another specific ideology.

But even in these cases, which fill me with anger, magic works its miracles, and the elusive capacity for generating new knowledge that a narrative triggers, transcends its meaning and elevates it to dimensions that cannot be Weaponised; The allegorical path chosen by humans to discover the truth of life surpasses both its author and its recipient. The content becomes a vehicle for a message beyond the writer's own intentions.

I cannot say that children's literature is intended solely for children. Nor can I truthfully say that when I write, I write only for those little people. Likewise, it would not be entirely honest if I did not say that when I write, it is to question myself and share with the world that life is a mystery of which I can better understand with the help of a story.

The **Medway** is a river located in the southeast of England. Its basin houses one of the most beautiful and lush landscapes in the United Kingdom. It gave its name to a significant battle in the 1st century, which was crucial for the arrival of the Romans to the great island of Britain. It has lent its name to a Unitary Authority which is akin to a region or conglomeration of towns within the country.

River Medway flows into the estuary of the Thames. Along its course, it passes through the magnificent landscape known as the "Garden of England": a well-deserved nickname due to its beautiful fields and intricate gardens, highlighting the English taste for floral decorations. The vibrant colours of its valleys and gardens are enhanced by the explosion of fragrances, and they harmoniously host countless animals and creatures of all shapes and sizes.

The historical legacy of this area, represented by grand castles and the architecture that can be seen in towns like Canterbury, Tonbridge, Sevenoaks, or Tunbridge Wells, makes it even more attractive and picturesque.

History and nature converge in this landscape, synthesizing beauty and modernity with tradition and harmony in a unique and often incomparable way.

Observation has been the primary feature that has enabled most of the advances in human history. By continuously observing nature, what gradually came to be called "Science" was developed.

In the past, looking up and observing the sky allowed us to read the heavens and helped us navigate through it. This Let us surpass beyond our small-mindedness and led us to encounter others: we could learn about different cultures and share different lifestyles.

Looking inward, the introspection of one's inner self, allowed us to scrutinize the human soul and dig into the very depths of our being. We could gain a greater understanding of ourselves and of the various social behaviours that shape our individual and social realities.

Observation has been the *alma mater* that gave content to each and every one of the stories that make up this book you now hold in your hands.

In **"The Medway Tales,"** you will immerse yourself in a collection of seven stories, each entirely distinct, yet simultaneously guided in a uniform direction. These stories originate from observing and savouring of the life that surrounds us.

Set in the adorned area bathed by the Medway, they share a common theme of human behaviour with a very profound anthropological foundation, which, while it could be called universal, is viewed from a very specific and powerful conception of the human being: we are called to be much more than we perceive of ourselves.

I hope you enjoy them as much as or even more than your children, for whom these stories have been created. Please, leave them with me now. I will tell them the same story, but this time in their own tongue.

To You, Our Dear Little Ones:

Hello, my friends!

The world is so big and it's a wonder, but you must understand it. If you know how to look closely, it's full of stories and adventures. Not all grown-ups understand them, but you do.

I invite you to get to know all these stories and to explain them to the adults, so they grasp the essence of life. That's what I call **children's literature.**

This book is called "the Medway tales" because these stories happen around the river Medway. It is in the southeast of a country called the United Kingdom. Go to a map and look for it. You may need the help of an adult, so ask for it.

This river flows almost in the same area as another super important river called the Thames, after passing through London. Have you found it?

The **Medway River** crosses what people call the Garden of England, an enormous place full of trees and plants of all kinds. Hundreds of different animals live there peacefully, unbothered by humans and their bustling lives.

One night soon, ask the adult beside you to take you out of the city where there are no lights. Look up: make sure there are no clouds that day. You'll be able to see hundreds of stars. The more you pay attention, the more you will see. We call that **"observing"** because you perceive things that have always been there, but you hadn't realized until that moment.

These stories that you are about to read come from observing the world and its inhabitants closely. Remember: the more you pay attention, the more you see.

Enjoy these seven stories. And when you finish, tell me which one you liked the most.

Santos CS Bermejo

Señor Huevo

"Not all that glitters is gold"

One early morning, Señor Huevo was, as always, walking toward the stream. His tiny little eyes, his slender little arms, his short little legs, his well-trimmed moustache, and a brown hat with a white chicken feather placed neatly on his little head.

Señor Huevo was an egg. However, not just a common egg. Señor Huevo was the most beloved and popular egg ever seen in the distant Aran Islands. Friendly, attentive, affectionate, and playful, he skipped up and down the hills, always whistling and singing his song full of cheer:

Señor Huevo says hello, with cheerful glo-o-o-o-w,
A great buddy and good neighbour, as you kno-o-o-o-w,
Come and join us, let our friendship brightly gro-o-o-o-w,
It doesn't matter who you are because we'll flo-o-o-o-w!

So, whistling and singing, Señor Huevo walked, distracted and pondering, when suddenly -crash! He stumbled on a little stone from the path.

Señor Huevo spun and spun. He rolled and rolled, and neither his short legs nor his tiny arms could stop him. He kept on rolling and spinning, turning around and around, until he thought that he could never get up on his own.

He heard a little kitten approaching from afar. So affectionate! So soft! So cute! So friendly! Silently, the kitten tried to sneak around Señor Huevo without saying a word.

"Please, kind kitty, I beg you: lend me a hand and help me stand."

"I wish I could, Señor Huevo!" said the good cat. "My owners are on their way, and when they enter the house, I must stay at the door to welcome them."

And this happy cat continued on its way, while Señor Huevo kept spinning and spinning, rolling and rolling, unable to stop himself.

Suddenly, he heard someone bark.

"Please, good dog, I beg you: give me a hand and help me stand."

" Señor Huevo, you know I can't. Sheepdogs are always on a mission.

 My sheep are waiting for me, and without me, they wouldn't know where to go. Who would protect them if I weren't there?"

 So hardworking! So responsible! So loyal! So diligent!

The little dog circled around Señor Huevo and continued walking along that rocky road.

As Señor Huevo kept turning and twisting, he lost hope of ever getting up. Suddenly, he heard subtle footsteps in the distance. It was a hamster who had just finished his daily exercises on his training wheel. So active! So cheerful! So diligent! So playful!

"Please, dear hamster, I beg you: give me a hand and help me stand."

"I would love to, Señor Huevo, to be able to move and have the strength to lift you up! I've been on my wheel for hours; I'm exhausted, defeated and super tired. How could someone so tiny lift someone as heavy as you?"

And off went that hamster in search of a bed to rest.

It was about to get dark. Señor Huevo kept spinning and spinning. He wanted to reach the stream to drink some fresh water and collect the wool that he would use to knit a cozy sweater.

"Oh, how warm the sweater I'll make with this Aran wool will be!" Señor Huevo thought as he spun and spun.

Then, he spotted one of those ugly, stinky hyenas that wander around without a care. So treacherous! So selfish! So dangerous! So malicious!

"Good day, mysterious traveller of the road. Do you need my help, my dear friend?" asked the hyena, smiling as she sniffed with her snout.

In an instant, Señor Huevo opened his eyes and breathed a sigh of relief. He felt very grateful as she helped him to stand up. The hyena and the egg, now friends, sang:

Señor Huevo and the hyena, a cheerful glo-o-o-w,
They're good buddies and great neighbours, as you kno-o-o-w,
Come and join us, let our friendship brightly gro-o-o-w,
It doesn't matter who you are because we'll flo-o-o-w!

And that's how the story of Señor Huevo comes to an end. From that moment on, he wasn't scared of falling at all. He knew he had a special friend who would be there whenever he needed Help.

Do not judge upon first sight,
as it's an illusion, not quite right.
For appearances can deceive,
look beyond the surface, take your time.

It's the magic of learning, you know:
if they help, let your gratitude show.
For those who don't, don't be unkind,
like Señor Huevo, keep an open mind.

Someone may seem calm or serene,
cheerful, mild, or full of glee.
Yet someone else may not appear,

repugnant, rude, or insincere.

So, keep in mind, my little friend:
don't just look at what they say,
it's how they act throughout the day.
True friends are those who show they care,
with actions kind and love to share.

Cheeky Little Mole Tillo

"Everyone comes to their day of reckoning"

Under a robust quince tree, lived Tillo, happy and free.
Dressed in blue from head to knee, and as lively as can be.
In the morning by the sea, afternoon with cup of tea,
playing board games in the eve, at night watching CBeebies.

His friend Duck came to read stories, poems, tales and children's books.
Tillo hid his in a flush, instead he wanted to cook.
Afterwards, Mr Cat longed to paint bright and bold pictures.
Tillo, in anger, turned around, bounded to his grinder and mixers.

One day, a squirrel came along to play 'tag' with little mole.
So excited, he took a glance, looking through the peep-hole.
But Tillo cried out, "Not outside." I'm too slow and it's so cold,
I'm not playing your silly tag; instead, I'll watch the Super Bowl".

His friend, the hog, dropped by, a bright warm morning last summer
to watch Peppa Pig all day long and eat creamy peanut butter.
But Tillo, as angry as he was, snatched the remote controller.
He shouted, "Paw Patrol, I said," like usually does to his brother.

One serene hot afternoon, came his friend Harriet the Goat
to ride the bike and see the lake or even sail her rusty boat.
Tillo made up some excuses, like he couldn't find his coat.
He remained alone at home, then decided to dig a moat.

A boiling summer afternoon, Leah invited him to a pool:
"Come on Tillo! Play with us. Join us; we have plenty of room!
Let's spend the afternoon together. We will play, splash and stay cool."
"I'd rather do some writing, Leah, and be prepared for the school."

Bouncy and playful, our Tillo, he truly obeyed Mr. Potts,
but at school was rather bossy, with friends he always call the shots.
He played pirates, cards and Uno, robots, nurses, ice-cream shops,
Keen on music, breaks and clubs, nothing more but playing tops.

The chameleon mailman came, one day and rang the bell's sweet chime,
with a cardboard parcel in hand, from the post and just on time.
Tillo snatched the parcel swiftly, just before any other friend,
wanting to unveil the treasure, from the Amazon, itself.

At night with his dad, as bedtime was near,
 a story or a tale, he would eagerly hear.
With joy and a smile, if the tale was just right,
but a frown would appear if it didn't fit his night.

COLEG
CATO

But one day inside his den
silence broke through, weirdly intense.
Meerkat Paco, suddenly came,
"This is a robbery, get on the ground!
Everyone quiet, don't make a sound!"
The meerkat shouted out loud,
Ev'ryone frightened, he found.
He took all toys, junk and pounds
All his belongings and lost-&-founds.

So, Tillo, alone, was left,
as empty inside as his den.
He set off to find his friends,
To see if they'd share
their toys and games.

He first looked for goat Harriet, to play with her bike or her boat.
But she was a bit busy now, finishing digging the moat.

After, he bumped into Leah, and asked her to go to her pool,
who also was busy by then, meeting her cousin on Zoom.

He looked for the Cat a bit later, and longed for reading a book,
who now with different people, was gone and enjoying the cook.

Annoyed, he looked for the Squirrel, he dressed up and put on his hat,
who now was noisily laughing, while playing her favourite tag.

Defeated and so very tired, Tillo felt gloomy and alone.
Not even could he watch TV, with his famous friend, the hog.

* * * * * * * * * *

Thus,
life treats you as you treat others,
if you share, people respond,
if you don't, expect the same,
but we learn how to overcome.

Luckily,
Tillo had Friends,
those ones, who no one deserves.
When some brief few days passed by
they came back with so much care.

Hyena Helena and the Mink Scarf

"You can't make a silk purse out of a sow's ear"

Once upon a time, there was a hyena named Helena.
Helena worked at the supermarket in the mornings, assisted her father at the butcher's shop in the afternoons, and delivered pizzas in her free time. Helena was super hardworking. She only rested on Sundays, which she even used for delivering letters and flyers to earn a little extra money.

"Why work so much?" you might wonder.

Helena had a secret: she wanted to buy a scarf.

Yes! A scarf! However, not just any scarf. A mink scarf! A luxurious mink scarf! A showy mink scarf to wrap around her neck. She wanted to appear in front of her friends, all dressed up, sophisticated, elegant, refined, and very distinguished.

Carnicería

Three years, five months, and two days working nonstop. That was the time it took for Helena to save all the money she needed to buy her fluffy, puffy mink scarf. And, in the end, she succeeded.

One sunny morning, she left her home and headed to the store where she had spotted that lovely scarf so many times. She went inside, bought it, and wrapped it around her neck not just once, not twice, not even thrice, but four times – that's how long it was!

Helena thought everyone was admiring her in her beautiful scarf. However, the truth was that no one was even acknowledging her.

You might wonder: 'What did Helena do when she got her precious scarf?'
Well, she went to the savannah. She wanted to impress the lion Nico and
his young lion pals. She paraded in front of them, spun around, showing
off her beautiful scarf.

But the truth was that the lions couldn't help but laugh behind her back
because they had a beautiful mane, much more splendid than that scarf.
Besides, they had had theirs from birth, naturally wrapped around their
necks, and how majestic they looked!

"You're not impressing anyone here," one day her dear friend said, "but
if you want to look a little more like us with your mink-mane scarf, you're
most welcome!"

So sad!

Helena didn't impress anyone on the savannah with her scarf. She was just like everyone else. So, the hyena moved to the forest to impress Manolo the fox and his friends, the little foxes.

She went up and down the castle hill constantly, parading in front of the fox dens, hoping they would see her shine with her mink scarf.

But, in truth, they were laughing at Helena behind her back. They had tails much fancier and showier than that mink scarf. Oh, how splendid those fox tails looked!

"Listen, Helena," one day, her good friend Manolo the fox said, "here, you're not impressing anyone. But if you want to be a bit more like us with your mink scarf-tail, well, you are most welcome! You could pass as one of us."

That saddened Helena greatly. She didn't want to be just like everyone else; she wanted to be different and original. Therefore, she decided to return home.

On her way back, she journeyed through the desert and stumbled upon Fulgencio the camel. She draped the scarf around her neck and proudly marched in front of him.

"Hello, Fulgencio. Do you like it?" said the hyena. "I can lend it to you if you like. Try it on, just a little," Helena suggested to the camel as she wrapped the scarf around his lengthy neck.

Not even one minute did the camel last with that warm scarf! He took it off immediately, saying, "Ufff! It's so hot! What's a scarf even doing in a desert?"

No one was interested. Not even the most hardened camel was impressed by Helena's mink scarf.

This saddened Helena very much. Then, she saw a meerkat approaching from afar. She wanted to give the mink scarf to the strange, peculiar, and rather ugly animal.

"Here, I'll give it to you. At least you'll look a bit more sophisticated," said the hyena.

"I don't need to pretend," the meerkat replied firmly. "Besides, I have everything I need." He seemed very sure of himself.

"You? You have everything you need?" Helena reproached him. She was astonished to see that he seemed like such a needy animal, and then, she burst out laughing.

She laughed non-stop, in fits of laughter, as only hyenas know how to. She couldn't stop laughing. She was rolling on the ground with laughter.

That booming laughter certainly impressed the meerkat. The camel was also quite amazed. "How amusing this hyena is!" thought the two of them. The word spread throughout the entire place. Animals from afar came to see the hyena rolling on the ground with laughter. Lion Nico approached too. So did the fox Manolo. Animals from all around came to admire her. How unique and peculiar this hyena was! What a contagious laugh!

Moral:

Trying hard to be like the crowd,
can make you feel lost, not proud.
But inside you, there's a special view,
that's your unique, amazing you!

Amik, the Architect

"Stay under truth's arm, and she will protect you from harm".

For those endless Saturday afternoons of Blue Planet
and David Attenborough with crisps
(October 2021).

In a hush, all the birds and fish fell silent: shhh.

Every little creature on the plain grew quiet at once and hid right away:
some behind the tree trunks, others amidst the branches, the mice dug
down to the roots, the frogs leaped into the creek's waters, and those with
wings took to the sky.

The forest went silent all of a sudden.

Among the rocks, some chubby and adorable cheeks peeked out. Attached
to them, a super tiny nose that could sniff out everything that was to
come. Soon, tiny yet wide-open eyes appeared, looking in all directions.
Later on, a plump and soft little body revealed itself, as fluffy as a cushion:
its hands like those of a raccoon, its feet like ducks, and its tail... Huh??
For a tail, it had a paddle, a racket, a fin, a palmetto, an oar, a rudder!!!

"Forward, everyone! The coast is clear!" urged Amik the beaver, glancing at his wife, Algonquina, and their two children, who were walking behind. "I'm really tired!" one of them complained.

"This wind won't let me take another step!" the other one groaned, exhausted.

"The wind is never kind when you don't know where you're going," their father reassured them, "but I believe we've arrived, and from now on, this will be our home."

Amik and Algonquina exchanged glances. It was the third time the couple had moved in their twenty years together. This open field seemed just perfect.

But...

Suddenly, a little noise from afar caught everyone's attention. They all started looking around eagerly, trying to find the source of that sound, as if it were the most important thing in the world.

"Where is it coming from?" one of them asked.

"Look!" the other one responded. "There's a group of alders and cherry trees over there! It must be coming from beneath their roots."

A small stream flowed among the trees. What a beautiful little creek!

"Quick, there's no time to waste!" urged Amik. "Besides, it's getting late, and it's dinner time, so let's get to work! Those who don't eat won't work, but if you want to eat, you have to get moving."

Everyone started gnawing as much and as fast as they could. They needed to make that noise stop. They had to put an end to the flowing water. Soon, twigs and leaves, small logs, and sticks began to pile up along the creek's edge.

Amik began building a dam to stop the flow. He gave instructions on where and how to place each twig. The whole family was working with a common goal: to stop that little stream's noise.

"I'm full now," one of the children said, filled from all the chewing.

"Me too," added the other.

"Quiet! Shhh," ordered Amik. "Listen! You can still hear the water flowing, though it's quieter now. Well, it's time to rest. That will be tomorrow's business."

They all went to sleep.

The next morning...

Surprise!!!

The little stream from the day before had turned into a big river. The water had risen, and now it looked more like a small pond. Many animals woke up early to see that their plain had turned into a pond. The dam stopped the water's flow, and the water held back, turning into a swamp. It had been like a miracle, all thanks to the barrier the beavers had made, which almost blocked the water's flow.

Many more animals came to the place, and upon seeing it, they decided to stay there forever, in this bustling hub of life.

"Good morning, beloved family!" Amik cried just getting up, as he yawned and stretched. At the same time, the other beavers came out from the burrow made of branches and gnawed logs from the night before.

"The water is still flowing, and I'm hungry," continued Amik. "Let's get to work! Those who don't enjoy working will end up working without joy."

And the four beavers began to have breakfast with those same twigs and logs they were placing in the dam. Gradually, they completely blocked the water. By stopping the river's flow, they created a beautiful wetland.

The more water there was in the pond, the more fish came to live in it. As the water rose, more plants, bushes, and trees grew around it. The more trees and fish that appeared, the more birds came to build their nests in that place.

You couldn't find any squirrel or frog,
nor a turtle, mouse, or any toad
that didn't want to stay, you see,
in the beaver's forest, wild and free.

Owls and salamanders, what a crew!
Salmons, eagles, finding their debut.
Elks and reindeers joined the art,
in the beaver's forest, with rhythmic hearts.

A drum of harmony, bold and bright,
progress and joy, in the forest's light.
All synchronized with cheerful glee,
By hardworking beavers, full of esprit.

You could see in life like in a forest,
there are those who lend a helping hand.
They work together and cheer along,
to make everything and everyone strong.

Wolves, coyotes, and foxes so sly,
Arrived quickly, oh my, oh my!
But that's a story for another day,
For now, our tale must fade away.

This Little Squirrel Called Rita

"Actions speak louder than words"

On the slope of the long-abandoned castle, the always cheerful little Squirrel Rita lived happily.

Rita was joyful, fun, remarkably nimble, and ever cheerful.

Every morning, Rita liked to look for the freshest valley nuts. What a glutton she was! She enjoyed ascending and descending trees, climbing, scaling heights, and slipping through the cobblestone fence, leading to the stream! She never stopped running back and forth alongside that creek encircling the castle hill.

"Good morning, little dove," Rita would say when passing by of her neighbours, the pigeons.

She always received the same response: a melodic coo - 'Brugrbr, brugrbr' - as they bobbed their fluffy necks forwards and backwards.

"Good morning, little birdie!" chirped Squirrel Rita, one day. "Since you live up high near the clouds, do you think it will rain today?"

The dove replied, "Brugrbr, brugrbr."

So, Rita went to the park without an umbrella to find nuts and play with her friends.

Suddenly, it started to drizzle, then rain, and even thunder. Poor Rita had to hurry back home, soaked to the bone from the rain.

"Good morning, little birdie," said Squirrel Rita the next day. "Since you woke up early to see the sun, did it tell you if it would be cold today?"

Her neighbour replied as usual: "Brugrbr, brugrbr."

Rita stared at the dove. She tilted her head to one side and then the other. She blinked and, without even a coat, just as she was, off she went to the park to find fresh peanuts and jump and play tag with her friends.

She hadn't even reached the stream's fence when a very cold wind started blowing. It was so cold and icy that Rita had to hurry back home to light the fire and get warm.

Sitting by the cozy fire, watching the wood burn, Rita couldn't help but wonder: "Is it that they don't want to answer me? Maybe they don't understand me? Or is it that I can't understand them?"

"Good morning, little birdie," greeted Squirrel Rita again, the following day.

"Since you can see the mountains from up there, do you think it will snow today?"

The dove replied as always: "Brugrbr, brugrbr."

So, Rita dashed off to the stream without a scarf, without a hat, and without the skis that squirrels usually use when it snows.

But very soon… it began to snow! First lightly, then harder, and in just a few seconds, the whole hill was covered in snow and ice, so much that Rita was slipping and couldn't walk more than a few steps.

Sad and tired, she returned home.

Little by little, over time, Rita stopped greeting her neighbours, the doves.

 "They won't understand anything I say, anyway! What difference does it make to greet them or ask anything?" she thought.

Until, one day, the Fox of the Valley appeared.

Rita was playing and frolicking, when the fox surprised her in a sneaky attempt to catch her.

"What a yummy meal," he said.

"Help, help!" Rita yelled. "The fox is coming!"

"Nobody is listening," he replied.

"The fox is on the way!" she said louder. "Help, help!"

In the blink of an eye, an army of doves appeared, surrounding the fox. They started spinning and circling around him. One spin, two spins, three spins... round and round, again and again, until the fox, dizzy and disoriented, hurriedly ran away.

"Thank you, little doves!" gasped Rita. "Thank you for saving my life."

From that moment on,

it didn't matter

if the little squirrel felt understood or not,

she would greet her neighbours

as soon as she left her home.

Little Rita knew well

that they understood her,

even if "brugrbr, brugrbr" was the response

to her "good morning, little doves."

Water Eddies

"Brain is worth more than brawn"

Once upon a time, after a night when the rain fell nonstop, the morning sun shone brightly. The river's current roared with strength. And in the middle of that noise, there was Archer!

Archer was neither big nor small, neither tall nor short; he didn't appear strong or thin. He wore a serious yet joyful expression. He was very sharp, oh yes, very clever indeed.

Archer was a survivor. He was a brave and determined ant who spent half of his life travelling up and down the river, surfing the wild waters of the Kentish plain.

The other half of his life was spent underground, in his cozy anthill, practicing on his static surfboard, while winter passed.

Now, Archer was mentoring an apprentice called Lenny. He was on the shorter side, always smiling, and incredibly calm. You could say that Lenny was very laid-back. He enjoyed surfing a lot, but he loved spending time with his mentor (or should we say, his friend) even more.

Archer and Lenny, Lenny and Archer, spent countless hours on their surfboards. Archer gave instructions, and Lenny listened carefully. The master guided their downstream adventures, and the apprentice followed, without a fuss.

> "Maintain your balance," Archer advised. "Use your hand to help with your turn," he encouraged his pupil, determined to make him the second-best surfer on the Eden River.

> "When you hear the water roaring behind you, jump quickly; the wave is coming! Stand up! Ride that wave high up, all the way to the end!" he enthusiastically commanded as an inspiring mentor.

HAWAY BEACH
2022

How many times had Lenny been pushed over by those waters? How many times had he fallen off his surfboard? I don't know. Many. Just as many times as he had determinedly and cheerfully picked himself up and tried again. Whenever he fell, Archer was always there to teach him.

"Did you see why you fell?" Archer asked. "You saw that whirlpool of water, didn't you?"

"Yes, I did," Lenny replied, "but I made a mistake. I didn't realize it was a STUMBLING eddy."

"Exactly!" the teacher continued. "It was a stumbling eddy. These whirlpools are on the river's edge to confuse surfers and make them fall. They mislead, distract, and paralyze you. If you can't recognize them in time and pass by quickly, they can trap you for days and days," Archer explained to Lenny, "going round and round in circles, without getting anywhere."

Lenny nodded his head as if he had heard the same scolding many times.

"Up we go!"

They helped each other get back on their surfboards. "Let's go for it again. Let's take that little stream over there, and it will lead us to the source of the treasure," Archer suggested.

"What?!?!" Lenny exclaimed. "What did you say?" "The source of the treasure?" Lenny stared at his teacher. "What treasure?" he asked, with his eyes getting wider and wider. "There is a treasure source in the river, and you never told me about it?"
the curious student continued.

"Yes, of course," the teacher replied calmly.

"Let's go!"
Lenny shouted as he surfed down the
stream, determined to be the first to reach the treasure's
source.

"No, wait!" his teacher shouted. "There are whirlpools you don't know about! Wait, wait!"
Archer kept yelling.

"Catch me if you can," replied Lenny.

"I won't catch you; you'll fall first."

"Never, for I am the mighty Lenny."

"It'll pull you off your board, buddy."

"How?! Who dares challenge me?"

"That very one over there: the eddy."

Splash!!!
Lenny fell into the water again, in the middle of the river.
With Archer's help, he managed to stay afloat.

"Come on, climb up. Follow me, you're tired, we need to rest."

Archer guided his student to the other side of the river. The sound of water could be heard in the distance. Lenny got a little scared.

"A whirlpool!" he exclaimed, frightened.

"It's okay, keep following me. It's a BREATHING Eddy. These whirlpools are for resting," continued Archer explaining to his
pupil: "The water spins slowly, turning around and around, gently, step by step. It takes its time. It helps the surfer catch
their breath again."

After some time spent circling and resting in this breathing eddy, little Lenny remembered about the
treasure's source. Then, his eyes opened wide once again, and so did his mouth:

"The treasure!!!"

Off they went, both surfing downstream, in search of
that source that held the treasure.

Just a few minutes later, in the distance, our friends spotted a shining treasure.

How to get there? There was a two-metre pit that separated the treasure from the river.

"You follow me, Lenny," the teacher said.

"Be careful, it's a whirlpool," the frightened student warned.

"Don't be afraid, it's a LAUNCHER eddy."

"Launcher?" Lenny acted surprised.

"Yes, it will help us jump those two metres across the pit. Without the push from this whirlpool, we would never be able to reach the treasure," the teacher assured.

And so, scared and fearful but determined and trying to muster his courage, the student entered the whirlpool's eye with his teacher, and... one spin, two spins, three spins... With each turn, they went faster and faster. And one more spin. So fast, so fast that soon the two brave ants shot out like a launcher, surfing towards their treasure.
The effort was worth it!

As in rivers, in life

we encounter eddies

that we fight.

Some freeze our motion,

while others calm us all,

some push us forward

and make us strong.

Recognizing them is the key

to move ahead and set us free.

Little Rainy Things

"It's more blessed to give than to receive"

One, two, three. A, B, C.

Ailish, Beatrice, and Celeste were the three most fun-loving and cheerful little droplets you've ever seen. Always together, always running, always playing, and most importantly, always laughing.

Ailish was super tidy, always neat and organized; Beatrice was the sunshine of the group, always making everyone smile; Celeste was an explorer, curious about everything, learning from it all, and trying new things.

A, B, C. One, two, three.

Ailish, Beatrice, and Celeste lived happily on their fluffy cloud. They had always been happy together. Even though they liked to hang out with many other little droplets, they always ended the day together. Before bedtime, they loved sharing their adventures and all they had learned throughout the day.

"When I grow up, I'm going to look for the best puddle in the world to jump into," Ailish told her two friends one night. "I want a good puddle, big and deep, so that when I jump, it won't hurt me. I will be with lots of other little droplets like us. They told me that when it's time to rain, if you don't find a good puddle, you might fall anywhere. I don't want to get hurt when I jump! And I don't want to be alone!"

"I really want to have a parachute," Beatrice told her friends that day. "It will be so much fun!" she said to her little pals. "On the way down, I can meet lots of other droplets and talk, laugh, and play with them. It will be super-duper exciting! No matter where I land, I'm sure of one thing, my friends: I'll bring my parachute with me."

"And you, Celeste?" one of the little droplets asked her.

"Mmmmm… I don't know, to be honest. I'm just a tiny drop: a drop and nothing more. A drop is meant to fall, to dampen, to dissolve, to refresh… If I fall down from here, I suppose I'll return here again. I don't mind if I disappear; after all, that's why I was born. After falling and wetting the earth, the sun will make me go up again like steam."

The other two little drops were so amazed by Celeste's wise words: "I don't mind if I dissolve while falling; that's what I am supposed to do. After refreshing and nourishing the ground, the sun will call me to go up again." But they were so tired that their eyelids felt heavier than their curiosity, so they fell asleep.

The next morning, the day they had been waiting for finally came. Dark clouds quickly covered the sky. The sun played hide-and-seek for a little while, then the wind started to blow really fast, and the clouds above said to their little drops: "Let's go, everyone! Let's go! It's time to rain! Jump, jump! Your time has come! Let's make the Earth wet and happy!"

One. A. Ailish was the first to jump. Her puddle was ready. It was an adventure to descend, and when she landed, hundreds of friendly little drops welcomed her with laughter.

Two. B. Beatrice jumped headfirst; it was so much fun! She opened her parachute halfway down and had a great time floating down safely, just as she had planned and wanted.

Three. C. Celeste closed her eyes, counted to three, and took a deep breath for a moment. She felt excited because she didn't know what would happen next. With no fear at all, she let herself fall, ready for anything.

It was the first rain, a lovely sight,
some claim to be a pure delight.
Thanks to it, the earth did sigh,
as the town echoed with children spry.

These little drops are eager to live,
with adventures I haven't yet unveiled.
Ailish, Beatrice and Celeste wish you well,
as this tale, for now, comes to an end.

Santos CS Bermejo

Luisto+ Quintanar

About the Author

Santos CS Bermejo was born in the picturesque region of La Mancha, Spain, not far from where Cervantes once depicted Don Quixote battling windmills as giants centuries before. He obtained degrees in Philosophy and Theology, and after travelling the world, he eventually made England his home.

For him, storytelling, tales, and parables represent a vast repository of contained wisdom and serve as a privileged vessel for the transmission of knowledge and culture.

This is evident in his numerous contributions to both national and international anthologies and magazines, as well as in his latest Spanish children's books, "Hoja de caer" and "Cuentos del Medway."

Life and its mysteries led him to encounter Luisto+ Quintanar: a proper Manchego man, quixotic, artist, and adventurer. We owe the embellishment of these stories to him on account of his designs and intuition
In the final stage, Isabel Parrilla, Fatima Abbass, Holly Davidsen, and Amaryllis Furness contributed to ensure that this book was well-written in the language of Shakespeare.

Quote from the author

"Narrative is the most sublime way to gaze upon the world, understand reality, and explain life."
The author

www.ingramcontent.com/pod-product-compliance
Lightning Source LLC
Chambersburg PA
CBHW082123180726
48291CB00011B/2819